RiDiCULOUS WRITERS

Awesome Stories

Edited By Vicki Skelton

First published in Great Britain in 2020 by:

Young Writers
Remus House
Coltsfoot Drive
Peterborough
PE2 9BF
Telephone: 01733 890066
Website: www.youngwriters.co.uk

Printed and bound in the UK by BookPrintingUK
Website: www.bookprintinguk.com
YB0448K

FOREWORD

Ladies and gentlemen, boys and girls, roll up roll up to see the weirdest and wackiest creations the world of fiction has ever seen!

Young Writers presents to you the wonderful results of *Ridiculous Writers*, our latest competition for primary school pupils. We gave them the task of creating a crazy combo to give them a character or an object around which they could base their story. They picked an adjective or verb and a noun at random and the result is some super creations, along with the added bonus of reinforcing their grammar skills in a fun and engaging way.

But the fun didn't end there, oh no! Once they had their subject they had to write a story, with the added challenge of doing it in just **100 words!** I think you'll agree they've achieved that brilliantly – this book is jam-packed with wacky and wonderful tales.

Here at Young Writers we want to pass our love of the written word onto the next generation and what better way to do that than to celebrate their writing by publishing it in a book! We believe their confidence and love of creative writing will grow, and hopefully these young writers will one day be the authors of the future. An absorbing insight into the imagination of the young, we hope you will agree that this amazing anthology is one to delight the whole family again and again.

CONTENTS

Greta Dixon (9)	64
Ethan Shaw (8)	65
Megan Holder (9)	66
Olly Fletcher (9)	67
Ava McQueen (9)	68
Lily Wragg (8)	69
Aaron Ellis (11)	70
Lucas Wilson (10)	71
Jude Wilson (9)	72
Barley Musson (7)	73

Quwwat-Ul-Islam Girls' School, Forest Gate

Mehjabeen Kamran (11)	74
Farhat Hoque (11)	75
Sajeeha Sajjad (10)	76

St John's CE Primary School, Bierley

Amelia Harrison-Blezard (9)	77
Evie Theabould (10)	78
Mia Dutton (9)	79

St Patrick's Catholic Primary School, Heysham

Olivia Willett Stewart (9)	80
Kyle Mitchell (8)	81
Frankie Hobson (7)	82
Laura-Kate Barker (8)	83
Cheryl Bamford (9)	84
Keisha Gray (8)	85
Bob Howard (8)	86
William Featon (9)	87
Oliver Loughhead (9)	88
Zach Moorehouse (9)	89
Alicia Dyminski (9)	90
Nathan Allison (8)	91
Ruth Welch (8)	92
Eoghan Gurr (7)	93

Worth Valley Primary School, Keighley

Summer Widdop (9)	94
Seraphim Weston (10)	95
Gracie McDermid (9)	96
Faith Evans (10)	97
Alex Binns (11)	98
Katie Lund (10)	99
Lily Rose Perigo (10)	100
Caitlin Kendall (11)	101
Georgia Kershaw (11)	102
Darcy Carter (10)	103
Kaitlyn Smith (11)	104
Grace Halifax (10)	105
Sam Robb (10)	106
Casey Walker (11)	107
Paige Price (10)	108
Maisie Smith (9)	109
Courtnie Sinfield (10)	110
Tomas Smith (11)	111
Ellie Simpson (10)	112
Isabelle Whitaker (10)	113
Cody Morphet (11)	114
Demi Walton (9)	115
Kaine Foster-Smith (10)	116
Malachi Byrne (10)	117

THE
STORIES

Hypocrite Hand Sanitiser And Pooey Toilet Paper

"Toilet paper where are you?" shouted Hand Sanitiser.

"You can't find me!" shouted Toilet Paper. As Hand Sanitiser was chasing Toilet Paper she realised he stopped running. Then she saw poo all over Toilet Paper. "Toilet Paper, please use some hand sanitiser!"

"I will only use some if you use some too?"

"No!"

"Well then I won't use any," said Toilet Paper.

"I'll make you!" Suddenly, more pooey toilet paper came through the door. "I'm going to sanitise all of you!"

"Argh!" Then Hand Sanitiser got covered in sticky poo. "I will not wear hand sanitiser!" and that was that.

Nyla-Monay Edwards (10)

Aldborough Primary School, Ilford

The Lazy Ninja

Kakashi was sitting on his sofa watching Anime, when suddenly *peeew!* The screen shut off. He pulled out a book and began to read. The book was torn out of his hands by an over-excitable Naruto. "Get lost," muttered Kakashi.
"Not until you teach me karate!"
"Can't be bothered!"
"You're a ninja! Of course, you can be bothered."
"No I can't." He lay down and turned to face the backrest.
"Kakashi! Stop being lazy." Kakashi turned to face Naruto and threw a Jutso move at him. On doing so he promptly fell asleep.
"Wake up!" said Naruto.
"No!"

Yunus Khan (11)
Aldborough Primary School, Ilford

The Farting Superhero

"I'm here to save you!" shouted Super Sam.

"I called for Terrific Tom not Farty Sam," moaned the old lady.

"But I guess you'll do!" said the other lady.

"She took my toilet roll."

"I got it fair and square!" shouted the old one.

"Right there is only one way to solve this! You need to have a competition on who should have it!" suggested Sam.

"No!" they both shouted. Suddenly, Sam accidentally dropped the roll and when he tried to pick it up he farted onto the pack of toilet rolls. *Parp!* His cape flew off. "Oops," said Sam.

Samanta Islam (11)
Aldborough Primary School, Ilford

3

The Repeating, Burping Memory!

"Argh!" A girl shivers as she enters a stinky, abandoned hospital. She is clueless that she has entered the burping doctor's hospital. Emily is coldly waiting for the doctor until the hospital's burper burps. In a sudden Emily shakes and faints and finds herself in the burping chair. Emily's brain is sucked up and she loses her memory. She has now become a farting beast and her burping memory shakes the horrible, stinky burping history. Emily is now known as the new burping and farting doctor, who repeats the tragic history to those who hear the fart and burping memory...

Eshaal Naureen (11)
Aldborough Primary School, Ilford

The Beyblade

One night in Gotelem hotel a Beyblade fan went to do a poop in the toilet. He looked at the poop, "A poop emoji!" shouted the guy.

"Is there a problem?"

"You can talk? Probably I'm hallucinating, let's take a deep breath and wipe my butt!"

"No! Paper! What should I do? What will I do? Oh I know, I will wash my bum with water, all good!''

"Hey you," said Poop, "you like Beyblades?"

"Yup!"

"I can be your blade?" So they won contests and the championship league.

Dennis Svitojus (9)
Aldborough Primary School, Ilford

Gentle Goldie!

Goldie the gentle rat was bullied by the other rats because she was white and gold. Also, she was kind and gentle, unlike the other rats. Soon after, Goldie got fed up and decided to travel to space. Twinkling gold stars were peppered across the midnight sky. "It's gorgeous!" gasped Goldie, who was breath-taken. Goldie was so blown away that she crashed! Once Goldie got out she realised she was surrounded by multicoloured rats! Goldie was delighted especially because they respected her for who she was. Suddenly, there was a big crash! Who was that?

Sara Ahmed (11)
Aldborough Primary School, Ilford

6

Luke's Hairy Visit To The Museum

Luke was one day exploring a museum filled with scientific chemicals. He felt a chemical spill on his foot and announced, "Oh it's fine, it's just a little spill." Luke said the wrong thing because after a minute his foot started to grow hair. Hair was continuously growing quickly. He needed a cure! He travelled to 100 shops looking for a cure but yet to find it. At this point he was confused, then he unlocked his phone and searched for a scientist. Finally, he found one and explain what had happened and gets better after five days of searching.

Esa Khonat (10)

Aldborough Primary School, Ilford

Barracuda And Square

It was another match between Barracuda and Square. Barracuda was very confident because he always wins against Square. He blasted plasma at him from his eye and it didn't do a scratch. Barracuda was shocked. He started to train his powers then he was ready. The Square started to laugh at Barracuda. He didn't do anything but stare, then quickly blasted the biggest blast he has ever done. He did it so powerful, he didn't blast it away. But he completely shattered it to atoms. He just blinked. In his language that meant he was laughing. Then he went.

Faizaan Goga (10)
Aldborough Primary School, Ilford

A Butterfly Named 011

Once upon a time lived a butterfly named Eleven. She had travelled from upside-down to Planet Earth to meet her long-lost time travelling friend, Maxine. The problem was that she looked different from humans, she had wings. Bad people were chasing her, it was her Papa. She looked everywhere. Finally, she arrived at the last place she hadn't looked, America. There was Maxine her friend but she noticed her Papa, they were stalking her. This was war. Her friend's pet, the goofy canine, helped them fight them. I wonder who is going to win this battle.

Asha Kotecha (11)
Aldborough Primary School, Ilford

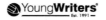
The Floating Toilet (With The Cat)

In a place called Tooting Cat, Mr Pieface was sitting on the loo. *Parp!* He farted and tooted while he was busy eating a Big Mac and watching James Charles. Suddenly, Mr Fat Nose stormed in while the cat was pooping potatoes. Mr Fat Nose had tentacles and levitated the toilet with Mr Pieface the cat on it but before he did he looked at the potatoes and Big Mac and said, "Don't mind if I do!" Then threw the toilet outside to the trash. Then James Charles came and said, "Hey sisters! We're putting make-up on today!"

Ayoub Mirza (10)
Aldborough Primary School, Ilford

The Gangster Wizard

Whilst rapping to his favourite song, The Gangsta Wizard was experimenting a silly spell. He mixes a spell that's called Silly, Willy, Dizzy spell that makes people rap to his favourite song Cardi B. How do they sing to his favourite song, you might ask. The answer is he has to speak to you. You would be rapping to his favourite song for five whole minutes but guess what the Silly, Willy, Dizzy spell didn't work. he was furious and wondered why it didn't work. He missed an ingredient, do you think he'll find the missing ingredient?

Ashtalfa Naureen (9)
Aldborough Primary School, Ilford

The Grubby Germ

Geremy jumped out of the bin. He had to find a hiding place. He couldn't hide in the fridge, his friends were there. He spotted a bubbling bowl of soup. He glanced at it carefully before hearing footsteps. Without thinking he jumped into it. *Toot!* His surroundings were now green. A large figure picked up the bowl and Geremy sprung in excitement. He was going on an adventure; his friends would never find him now. A large, metal boat picked him up and he saw a very pink cave opening. So he leapt and he climbed into someone's mouth.

Mehjabin Rahman (11)
Aldborough Primary School, Ilford

The Talking Chair

I came home from school and I sat on my favourite, pink chair. Suddenly, when I was reading my book, the chair yelled, "Why are you sitting on me?"
I leapt out of the chair. "You're a chair, built for sitting!"
The pink chair got angry. "I don't deserve to have people's bottoms on my beautiful face!" the chair screamed. Why had the chair got angry now, I had sat on it lots of times before. The pink chair had no face, where was the voice coming from? I never sat on the talking chair again...

Zara Boot (10)
Aldborough Primary School, Ilford

The Jealous Ice Cream

Once in a park was an ice cream van. The most popular flavour was mint. Mint was always showing off. Soon after, sprinkles were invented and put on a new ice cream. To Mint's misery, everyone preferred the new ice cream over him. No one bought him anymore, he was jealous. Realising Mint's jealousy, the new ice cream asked the server to put sprinkles on Mint, now he was happy. Not for long though because after a week, a new ice cream came along. He had a wafer! Now Mint was green because he is actually mint flavoured with jealousy!

Ayesha Islam (10)
Aldborough Primary School, Ilford

The Adventure Of The Spider-Fox!

Once upon a time, there was a Spider-Fox that just got his licence and ended up crashing into a boxing arena! The boxers were in the middle of a plan so they decided to stir up the plan. The boxers punched him so hard he managed to go through the ceiling and into space. The Spider-Fox met a magical football who definitely didn't like him. The magical football decided to get his magic wand and turn him into a football. The magical football then kicked him and he came back to Earth! Everybody was laughing, he couldn't handle it.

Winston Adjei (11)
Aldborough Primary School, Ilford

Evil Dr Pizza

There was a normal pizza who was used for a science experiment. He was dipped in radioactive fluids and became Evil Dr Pizza, with his sidekick Malcho Ketchup. He used every living organism as an experiment: does it taste good with Ketchup? Now French Frie embarks on a quest to defeat Evil Dr Pizza. Seeing this as a threat he captures the hero and nearly dips him in the acid, when he hears the funniest joke ever and laughs so much he farts the biggest fart in history and it propels him to another galaxy. Will we see him again?

Abdullah Ahmad (10)
Aldborough Primary School, Ilford

The Burping Brother

In the smelliest room lived The Burping Brother. The house smelled of burp all the time as the burping brother burped all the time. Everywhere he went people walked away because he never stopped burping. That was why he was called The Burping Brother. Everybody called his house the smelliest house in the village. Then one day The Burping Brother couldn't stand the smell of his house anymore, so he decided to take a bath. He went 'ew' and without any clothes on he ran out of his house. He lived happily ever after.

Devananda Pratheesh (8)
Aldborough Primary School, Ilford

The Forgetful Frying Pan!

Once in a filthy kitchen lived a forgetful frying pan, he wanted to visit a friend who lived in the bathroom. He packed his bags and travelled. When he was halfway in the hallway he encountered an unkind boot that kicked him back to the kitchen. He went back to where the boot was and kicked the boot somewhere. He forgot his shoes so travelled back home and got his shoes. He gave up searching for his friend. Suddenly, he was woken up by laughing in a cupboard. He went into the cupboard and inside was a fat, laughing llama.

Ashvin Shanti Kotecha (11)
Aldborough Primary School, Ilford

Poorly Rabbit

One morning there was a poorly rabbit, she cried so much she nearly vomited. She was so crazy she never ever went out of her house more than once a week because she thought she would get sick because the shops made her very sick. Every time she went into someone's house or in a shop, she would usually start vomiting, that's why she never went anywhere. One night she decided to leave the house and went to her new house. She started to vomit on the way back from her new house and never ever went back to her house.

Faziza Ahmed (9)
Aldborough Primary School, Ilford

Forgetful Scientist

One wonderful, forgetful morning he wanted to go to his unclean, dirty room. In his room was a rusty, old map. It was maybe his unforgetful thing. He took his magical stick and put it on himself and... He turned somewhere. He definitely forgot where the toilet was but why did he didn't forget the magical stick? Then later when he had a chat he needed the toilet, but what would he do? So he should have to ask but he was so eager he couldn't do anything. So he would only do his, you know what, his fart, forever.

Ema Kalinauskaite (9)
Aldborough Primary School, Ilford

Rude Toilet

One day I was washing my hands in the mall toilet. Then a man walked in and into the toilet. After a while, somebody was talking. It was the toilet! I was startled. I started to run but all the toilets were chasing me! After ten amazing minutes, I was whacked. Surprisingly I lost them. Meanwhile, the golden toilet king made a speech. "You are not made to be rude! You are nice! So show them who you are!" shouted the king. The toilets returned and treated them nicely. Then all the people went and had a smile!

Aarav Minhas (10)
Aldborough Primary School, Ilford

Evil Vomit Grows Legs For A While

One terrific, horrific morning in a quiet reception it was full of vomits but there was one evil one. He had horrible, scary eyes. He was incredibly smelly. Oh no! Then the vomit started to get legs and hands and started to run around the hotel with the stinky smell. It left footsteps. It slipped and accidentally disappeared. After he was found on the bed. He was very stinky and made the bed stinky. After that moment he was called the disgusting Evil Vomit and he was now very careful in humans' big bodies.

Maksimas Katinas (9)
Aldborough Primary School, Ilford

KFC

Once there was a rat named KFC. It was his dream to become a waiter. So one day he tried to serve some giants at the cafe but they fainted straight away. KFC didn't give up, he tried again the next day. Then he saw giants throwing up after their food. He went to the chef to complain but low and behold the chef was none other than a slug! He nearly peed. He asked the slug his name and then broke out laughing because his name was ludicrous. It was, 'I am a human, not a slug!'. Don't ask.

Anita Patel (11)
Aldborough Primary School, Ilford

The Destruction!

It is a normal day at Riverdale town and a boy who lives on a farm was waiting for an adventure. One day a mysterious creature came to the town and it was called Destruction and it was half rabbit and half robot. The boy was finally happy to have an adventure. The boy was dancing around. Destruction made a curse on the town and the boy went to stop him so he stopped at Destruction and forced him to make the town stop jumping and he did. Destruction was never to be seen again and the boy was a hero.

Amy Diagne (11)
Aldborough Primary School, Ilford

The Trumping Teacher

The smell of rotten egg and blue cheese came from stingray, it was Mr Blob farting. He was the stinkiest thing in England or the world! He didn't have any friends and all his students hated him. They always sat at the back of the room. Everybody wanted him to be fired, he was awfully stinky. One day, he did a burp but he didn't know what a burp was, so he slowly went towards his students and asked what a burp was. They all said it's not stinky like a fart then he only ever just burped.

Emily Patel (8)
Aldborough Primary School, Ilford

Clumsy Pineapple

Once when Clumsy Pineapple woke up he wanted some water, so he went to the kitchen. He went to get some water from the fridge but oops... Clumsy Pineapple split the water on the floor. He thought if he moved somewhere else he wouldn't fall down or be clumsy. He moved to The North Pole but it was so cold. So he told his friend to fly him to an island but it was too watery and he would fall down into the water! Then finally he found a place where he could relax and there he was in his world.

Yaseera Vesamia (9)
Aldborough Primary School, Ilford

The Goofy Llama!

One day the llama bumped into Mad Milk Man, he tried to say hello but it sounded like it was swearing. The Mad Man stormed away. The next day he went to the street, everyone looked the same as him. They spoke the same too. They sounded awful. He suddenly realised how bad he sounded. He needed to eat the saving apple to put everything right. He travelled and met 11 who helped him through the way. When he got to the saving apple he took a large bite and his teeth fell out! Bye goofiness...

Maya Shahid (11)

Aldborough Primary School, Ilford

The Supercalifragilisticexpialidocious Rat And Cat

One time in a year a rat and a famous rat met a normal human and he had a cat who was very buff and he took the human's pear. So Albert called his pet Meagoku. He was gonna eat the disgusting rat and he knew he was going to have to go because he stole the softest pear, it was the sweetest purest tastiest pear. He wouldn't take it. It was ludicrous and the Meagoku just ate him and he was going down his bumpy throat and got stuck and Meagoku died on the hard, dirty floor.

Maurylio Metzger (11)
Aldborough Primary School, Ilford

Angry Pizza

Once upon a time, there was an angry pizza. She sat on a shelf loudly. She wanted to steal the most delicious mustard, the yummy ketchup, the creamy cheese and the tasty sauce. The pizza was very greedy and lazy, she couldn't be bothered to wash the dishes. Also, she was rude, crazy and a very grumpy. The pizza was not even bothered to deliver someones pizza. Pizza couldn't speak English which was very weird. One day her friends told her off so pizza got so upset.

Valerie Adjei (11)
Aldborough Primary School, Ilford

The Rude Monster

In the deep, dark forest there was a gigantic, big and most sly monster in the world. He was in the most sluggish part of the forest and he wanted people to come into the sluggish part of the forest. Each day he would wait for someone to come so he could gobble them up, he never had to eat unless people came. A few moments later the monster saw many people coming to see him, he was proud because that time he knew he could eat people so he ate them up until he was full.

Kayden Wright-Thompson (7)
Aldborough Primary School, Ilford

The Clumsy Cat

One sunny morning, there was a seven-year-old girl who had a pet and that pet was a cat. Then one day the girl was setting out the food for the cat to eat (milk). After an hour the girl called the cat to drink the milk. While the cat was walking to its food, she was bumping into things. The cat was closing its eyes, thinking of a song and bumped into the wall. When the cat reached its food the cat accidentally split the milk. After, the cat was called the clumsy cat.

Nivedhi Jeyaram (10)
Aldborough Primary School, Ilford

The Lazy Wizard

A long time ago there lived a wizard. Every day he was busy making potions. One summer's shiny day he was as busy as always, making a potion to make people active. After all his hard work the wizard went to sleep. At night the potion accidentally fell on the wizard! In the morning he found out that he forgot to put something in the potion and he became not active, he became lazy. He was so lazy he never woke up! After that nobody saw the lazy wizard...

Valeria Rosca (9)
Aldborough Primary School, Ilford

The Crazy Teacher!

One rainy morning, the crazy teacher Lucan was teaching times tables to his students. "6x6=8 and 2x9=24 and 5x5=0," she said. After everyone went to lunch, Lucan went to sleep in the cupboard where all the students' books were and she squashed them. Later when she came out she made the students sneeze 600 times so she was known as the crazy teacher! She ate ice cream every day at school, so the classroom smelt like vanilla ice cream.

Safiyyah Bulbulia (9)
Aldborough Primary School, Ilford

The Evil Pizza (Revenge)

There once was a nice, amazing pizza until... The people that bought the pizza just threw it away! "Why me, now I'm so mouldy! I need revenge!" After that day, the pizza went to any house he could find and made the other foods mouldy! Until some food stood up for themselves. "Stop doing this, it's not worth it!" shouted the onion. The pizza understood what he had done wrong and turned everything back to normal.

Maria Lunga Vasite (9)
Aldborough Primary School, Ilford

The Monster

One lovely day a monster went to a shop to buy a cookie. At the shop, he got a cookie but when he went to pay he remembered that he forgot his money so he said, "May I have this cookie for free?"

The shop keeper said, "No! You have to pay." So the monster ran and ate all the cookies and flew away. A helicopter followed the monster, but then the monster saw it and farted all the way to space and landed on Jupiter.

Austeja Bickauskaite (10)
Aldborough Primary School, Ilford

The Terrifying Football

It was a Sunday afternoon and the team were going to play on a field. As they were playing on the field one of the kids went home and went on holiday to Turkey. He made a new friend and told him how to play football. He was going home and went back. He played really well and the manager said, "You play football and play well." They scored lots of goals. The coach said, "You have won the match." They had won the game.

Farhan Majeed (11)
Aldborough Primary School, Ilford

The Crazy Toilet

I was in the toilet minding my own business, then the toilet started shaking and took me in! After that, the toilet stole the person's personality and turned into G-T gangster toilet! Every time someone did waste, he would store the waste and fly and drop the waste out of the window.
Five years later he still continues the reunion at 65 years old and his grandchildren will carry G-T on forever and ever until they die.

Yuvraj Panesar (9)
Aldborough Primary School, Ilford

Sir Chef Wasterman

Chef Wasterman was the worst chef in the whole world. His favourite was burgers containing tree buns, human leg patties, bogey lettuce and diced blood tomatoes. His restaurant is called 'Yummy In My Tummy' where they rate it one star on Trip Advisor. Once he burnt a human leg patty and it was the last one but luckily his boss told him to kill someone and mince them. He did it and so he had 100 more human leg patties.

Aiven Skrodenis (10)
Aldborough Primary School, Ilford

The Jealous Superhero

Mark escaped from prison. He was very jealous because the villains were robbing the jewellery store so he joined them. When he joined them he realised that they hadn't given him any jewels so he snatched them off them. When he snatched them he went to the toilet and he accidentally dropped the jewels so he went in the toilet. Suddenly, he dropped into the toilet but he managed to escape with the bag full of jewels.

Ohona Pathan (10)

Aldborough Primary School, Ilford

The Burping Dinosaur

One day, a dinosaur was very hungry ad was a friendly guy. While he was looking for something to eat, something happened... He burped and he burped again. He fell down with a big bang. As soon as he got up, the dinosaur glimpsed and trekked along the narrow path and eventually saw a young, little, cute girl. Although the young child didn't know the dinosaur, she gave him a hug and they became friends.

Abigail Keen (10)
Aldborough Primary School, Ilford

The Talking Toilet

One day there was an old, talking toilet and nobody wanted to come and do their business on it. The talking toilet was very happy. There came an evil boy who wanted to smash the toilet. The toilet said, "Why do people have to do their stinky business in me!" The boy was sat on the toilet, the toilet blasted the boy up out of the window and he landed in a pile of poo.

Mahboub (11)
Aldborough Primary School, Ilford

Grecu

One morning, there was a hero and he went to his new school. When he entered everybody was bullying him and making fun of him. So he got very mad. One day he went back to school and people kept on making fun of him so he decided to jump on the tables and kick everything because he was so angry. So that day he went to school very angry, so everybody called him Angry Superhero.

Giulia Maria (9)
Aldborough Primary School, Ilford

The Burping Toilet And His Friend Cookie

"Haha," said the burping toilet. "I'm so happy, burp!"
"Stop!" said the cookie. "It smells and my taste is going to go so stop!" The toilet realised that the cookie was upset so he stopped burping on purpose and only burped when he needed to. This made the cookie happy because he stopped burping.

Lidia Maria Lungu (10)
Aldborough Primary School, Ilford

The Stinky Superhero

In a giant city there lived a stinky superhero, he was the stinkiest superhero in the whole of England. The superhero was so stinky he could scare any monster everywhere, he was so stinky. When the superhero fell asleep he sleepwalked to the bath and turned on the tap. He filled the whole bath with shampoo and he wasn't stinky anymore.

Herman Kola (7)
Aldborough Primary School, Ilford

The Sticky Chef In The Toilet

One day a chef was cleaning then he went to the toilet. The toilet started to fly all over the world. The sticky chef was so scared. Then the toilet fell. *Boom!* With a crash, *bam!* He fell but he did not die. Then he went to the hospital back to the restaurant to work, and he never dared to enter the toilet again.

Miraj Alam (10)
Aldborough Primary School, Ilford

The Hairy Chef

In the stinky, smelly, ginormous restaurant in England, the hairy chef had never had a hair cut in thirty years and he even left trails to the shop so he never got lost. Then he finally went to the barber to get his hair cut but the haircutter said, "I can't cut your hair, because it is too long, sorry!"

Hafsa Alam (8)
Aldborough Primary School, Ilford

The Polly Fly

One hot morning the Polly fly starting to feel very sick. She went to the doctor's and he said to stay in bed. After two days she didn't feel better, all she wanted was to feel better. She had chickenpox and was desperate for them to go away.

Afsana Dragoi (9)
Aldborough Primary School, Ilford

Jazzy Jungle

It all started in the jungle. Emma who was a detective travelled to the jungle. She could hear thuds of footsteps. She looked through her binoculars and to her surprise, she gazed and spotted a llamapug and a pandadog, the rarest creatures on Earth. Emma gasped. She got her camera out and took a picture. *But why in a jungle?* she thought. Anyway, she galloped over and heard something. She heard a voice. She realised it was the animals talking! She was so amazed she could faint but she didn't. It was her most valuable fortuitous, most extraordinary day.

Harleen Deol (10)
Our Lady Of Fatima Catholic Primary School, Birmingham

The Ice Cream King

Long ago at a time when dinosaurs roamed the Earth, actually, Wednesday 4th March 2020, there lived an ice cream king (his real name is Bob, but I guess that doesn't matter). He ruled over all ice cream. Mint, chocolate, strawberry, vanilla, everything. All until yesterday. He was confronted by the actual queen! They both had lived in the country Sploon for years, but they had never met each other. They had a secret meeting in a secret ice cream underground bunker (also known as ICUB). The ice cream king came out with bottom lip trembling, oh no!

Ariadne Crosby (10)
Our Lady Of Fatima Catholic Primary School, Birmingham

The Flying Pig

The world was dull... Until Zachary, the flying pig was born. He brought people great joy as he would perform for a huge crow and bring happiness to them. But soon, people began to dislike his regular routine and wanted to see bigger and better things. Zachary loved to make people happy but he was exhausted after a regular performance. How could he cope with the crowd's requests?! The pig's owner wanted the money so he forced Zachary to perform even though he was very tired. Will he be able to survive this horrible nightmare?!

Bradley Nduka (9)
Our Lady Of Fatima Catholic Primary School, Birmingham

Sassy Chicken

Sassy Chicken wears huge sunglasses so you can't see half of his face. His famous saying is "Don't you dare bring that sass!" in an American accent. He laughs like Maleficent and talks like Peppa Pig. Sassy Chicken looks around for someone all the time. One day he went the road to look for a nerd. The nerd was sitting on the bench doing some work, Sassy Chicken went up to him and said... But the nerd stood up and said, "I work to get a good job and not to be an Asda worker soon like you, ha!"

Hirah Haravi (10)

Our Lady Of Fatima Catholic Primary School, Birmingham

The Potato With Jelly Legs!

There once lived a potato, but not an ordinary potato. A potato with jelly legs! This potato was called Jerry, he was made fun of for being unable to walk. Every day he would try until couldn't anymore. (When he was tired). One day, something unbelievable happened. He did it! But not long after he was found and eaten. How sad! He didn't give up so you shouldn't too. Even though he is dead, he achieved his goal to walk. Which means you can too. Never give up on your dreams because one day it will happen.

Bronagh Speer (10)
Our Lady Of Fatima Catholic Primary School, Birmingham

The Fart Fairy

Once there was a Tooth Fairy. Then it was replaced by the Fart Fairy. Instead of taking your teeth, it takes your farts. It doesn't repay you with money it gives you stinkiness. When you wake up it makes you run from your room because of the smell. You could faint! If you find a pound when you lose a tooth it is the Tooth Fairy, if you smell farts in your room it is the Fart Fairy. In real life, nobody has seen the Fart Fairy because it is a big, green, smelly, ugly piece of someone's big fart.

Anna Benavidez (9)
Our Lady Of Fatima Catholic Primary School, Birmingham

Farting Pig

One day above the clouds was a pig that lived on a farm. He was the only pig on the farm. He was going to the vets to see if he had Fartobetes, he didn't want Fartobetes because if he did he would have to go to the dump. He went to the vets, he had to have an operation to see if he had Fartobetes. Two hours later, he had to go on a train to the dump. He was angry and did the smelliest fart ever which confirmed Fartobetes. *Puff, puff, puff!* He hit his head badly.

Dior-Wray Campbell (10)
Our Lady Of Fatima Catholic Primary School, Birmingham

The Stinky, Stanky Pizza

Many years ago a stinky pizza lived on Planet Stink-alot. One day he was exiled for not being stinky enough, so he went to Earth. *Splat!* He landed on the streets. Suddenly, stink clouds started appearing around him, then around buildings then around the whole world. Then, the stinky, stanky pizza felt a bit peckish so he snuck into a calm cafe. A few minutes later he realised he had eaten everything. A man was stomping towards the cafe and barged through the door. He asked for pizza. Then the pizza jumped on the table and the man ate him.

Jasper Musson (11)
Porchester Junior School, Carlton

The Rude Toilet

One day John went to McDonald's to get a cheeseburger. He had to go to the toilet. The rude toilet said, "You smell!" Then the toilet ate him up. Oh, no! The McDonald's worker had to go to the toilet, so she went, She saw the disgusting, rude toilet eating up the man so she ran and told the boss. The boss insisted that the place went on quarantine with everyone inside. Everyone was petrified and nervous. Everyone could only eat McDonald's. All the people lived the rest of their lives eating McDonald's and never leaving.

Owen Lewis (10)
Porchester Junior School, Carlton

The Clumsy Dinosaur

Once upon a beetroot, a clumsy Diplodocus slips on a banana into the milky lake. He washed up on the biscuit shore. The giant dinosaur walked by a Hobnob hut. Diplodocus the Diplodocus fell over and an Oreo mammoth helped him get up. They went through the Curly Wurly jungle and made it to the choco desert, then the two sawm through the juice river. Now at the dark chocolate jungle, they walked through it and past the gummy, grizzly bear. Suddenly, the burger giant attacked but the team managed to run all the way to the dino's home. Yay!

William Hardisty (10)
Porchester Junior School, Carlton

The Forgetful Pizza

One day, there was a forgetful pizza. He was eating delicious fries. A few hours later, the forgetful pizza fell asleep in his bed watching his iPhone. He had the craziest dream ever. In his crazy dream, his whole house fell into space. When he fell into space he landed on a planet called Pizza Land where there were pizzas eating dirty raw onions. He forgot where he was and forgot what pizzas were. After his dream, he woke up and had fries stuck to him because he forgot he was eating oily fries while watching his smashed and cracked iPhone.

Layla Hand (8)
Porchester Junior School, Carlton

The Evil Football

One night the table footballers came to life but they had a big match ahead of them. Red table vs blue table. They kicked off but at that moment the ball was kicked the red team's players had gone. Then the ball was going in until Evil Football curled himself out of the way. Nineteen other players have died and it was a 1 V 1 (both goalkeepers) Then the Evil Football bit the red team's goalkeeper's T-shirt off. When the fans started to leave, blue team's goalkeeper hit the ball so hard the ball went out of the stadium.

Ben Meades (10)
Porchester Junior School, Carlton

Ludley The Forgetful Rabbit

This may sound ridiculous, but one day a suspicious, ordinary rabbit saw a carrot truck and ran like the wind but didn't look where he was going and hit a tree and forgot everything including where his burrow was. He lay there for hours. Suddenly, he imagined that there was a pink unicorn trying to eat him and ran into the forest like a headless chicken and scurried into a random burrow. He did not realise that is was a drain! He glanced down the vast hole and saw lots of ice cream licking spiders dancing and partying! Crazy!

Zach Giles (10)
Porchester Junior School, Carlton

The Rude Doctor

There lived a rude doctor. He screamed in all the patients' faces until they were unconscious. The few months of being hired the boss of the hospital used his huge magical boot to fire him and kick him out. It was a magical boot since it could kick people to space. From space, he fell down to ground until he was unconscious. After an hour, the rude doctor decided he'd be a rude robber. He started to scream in the shop keepers' faces until they gave him all their money. But one day the police saw him and arrested him.

Taran Sandhu (9)
Porchester Junior School, Carlton

Stinky Days

Once there was a scientist and he was very smelly. One day he went to a farm to do an experiment. Afterwards, the scientist was looking at the chickens then he fell into the pig mud, it stunk. Unfortunately, the shower water ran out so he smells. Luckily the showers start working again but instead of water, it was swamp water. The scientist was so cross he started to wash himself in the pond. After nine months he collected flies in his beard and his hair. After a year the normal water came back as rainwater, could it get worse?

Isaac Westby (9)
Porchester Junior School, Carlton

Burping/Farting Scientist

This may sound ridiculous for a scientist but did you know scientists let the gas out too. This was no ordinary scientist letting gas out. This was the scientist who trumped and it changed the colour of the liquid in the experiment he was doing and when he burped it sucked up the science tubes. He became very fat and every time he spoke you could see the science tubes down his throat. Then he did another massive burp and the tubes came shooting out of his throat. Trust me it was disgusting, he even used the same tubes again.

Jasmine Hoult (10)
Porchester Junior School, Carlton

The Toilet

Once upon a time, there was a magical toilet who loved highlighters and eggs. He had a whole stack of them. Then one day they disappeared. A muscular lion came to help him find them! This was hard work so they ate a hairy pineapple, a pickled toad and a slimy pumpkin for lunch. When they got up they both tripped over a vase on the floor and the slipped over some jelly from years ago. They both had to go to the hairy hospital. When they finally got better they put on some cool sunglasses and enjoyed the rain.

Greta Dixon (9)
Porchester Junior School, Carlton

Clumsy Football

This is no ordinary football! Somehow it's clumsy! Once someone gave it a very gentle kick and it flew down the pitch, for some reason it always hit its face. Then someone gave it a strong kick and it went far off the pitch where no one could see it. It turns out it flew 752 metres in front. After this, it was put in the hospital for balls. On the way in the ball saw screeching tennis balls and screaming basketballs having smelly air coming out and much more. The football felt the bed and fell asleep.

Ethan Shaw (8)

Porchester Junior School, Carlton

The Hungry Robber

Once upon a dark night, there was a hungry robber. This may sound ridiculous but instead of keeping the money and using it, he eats it! One day the hungry robber had an idea! He would get a plane and go all around the world and see how much money he could eat from those banks! The hungry robber went to France, Spain, Canada and even Australia. But, the hungry robber was still hungry! But he had also stolen all the money from the world. So, he pooped out all the money again for the banks. No one took it.

Megan Holder (9)
Porchester Junior School, Carlton

The Cyborg Ice Cream/Pizza!

One day there lived a Cyborg Ice Cream Pizza or known as CIP. CIP lived in a nostril village. One fine day, CIP started to melt. CIP found a wizard with a bumhead, he knew where some sprinkles were to make CIP never melt again. The wizard wanted something in exchange, that something was a toilet with a head inside. Alter that day CIP got the toilet with the head inside and gave it to the wizard. The wizard gave the sprinkles and CIP put them on. The next day, there was a black hole so CIP died anyway.

Olly Fletcher (9)
Porchester Junior School, Carlton

The Terrifying Dinosaur

Once upon a time, there lived a boy called Ronald. He wanted to go on holiday with his family to Jupiter and his alien mum and vampire dad agreed to go on holiday. They went on a Big Mac plane and stayed in a huge brick bedroom in a hotel that's one star on Jupiter. On their second day of being on Jupiter, they met a dinosaur who was so, so terrifying and ate cat food for dinner and played lots of games. On the day they left they all went back to Earth, even the dinosaur.

Ava McQueen (9)
Porchester Junior School, Carlton

How The Hungry Toilet Never Ate Again!

Once upon a poo, there was a toilet that loved searching the trash for food! But one sunny, happy day he saw green vegetable monsters. They were eating all his food. But... he hated green vegetables. So he tried one and he thought it was disgusting but they ate his nice food so he ate them all for his precious food. So after he ate all there crumbs. He didn't realise that he ate all them in a flash. So that's what made him so he never, ever ate ever again!

Lily Wragg (8)
Porchester Junior School, Carlton

A Very Hungry Foot

A long way away from Earth there is a very hungry foot. The foot lived on the planet Shoe and once it got so hungry that it started to eat Shoe. It started with a forest, then a mountain, then a massive statue of King Burger. This foot wasn't nice and they had to call their grateful wizard Hairy Toilet. This toilet was very, very hairy, he went to the foot and said stop, then suddenly, he was eaten. Then the foot pooped it all out.

Aaron Ellis (11)
Porchester Junior School, Carlton

Farting Ghost

The Farting Ghost had diarrhoea and got it on a man when he was in the toilet. He once pooed and it splattered in the tiles on the roof and on his face. He met a cow with a vest on and he had an aeroplane which was parked on a curb. Farting Ghost was on the toilet and fell into the toilet where he met a nose with wings and it started to fire bogeys at him and they were brown. The farting ghost aimed his bum at him and started firing.

Lucas Wilson (10)
Porchester Junior School, Carlton

Millionaire Brick

There was a millionaire brick that lived on Mars where every object is alive. One day a dragon came and gobbled up the millionaire brick. Somehow the millionaire brick turned into a teddy bear and the dragon spat it out. It exploded leaving a line of rainbow stars and from then on his new name was Millionaire Teddy Bear. He still had 10,000 pounds because that was the only thing that mattered to him.

Jude Wilson (9)
Porchester Junior School, Carlton

Gangsta Pizza Party

It happened when everyone went home. It threw cheese and tomato everywhere and made an army of gangsta pizzas and they made everything pizza. One day some of them got arrested. The others made a rescue plan and they jumped out and rescued the gangsta pizzas.

Barley Musson (7)
Porchester Junior School, Carlton

The Burping Superhero

There once lived a burping superhero, who always burped and that is how he made his villains faint. His burps were as loud as an elephant blowing through its trumpet. One day he was fighting a villain in the beautiful town called Sundried City. The villain was called The Cackler. So the superhero burped but it didn't work because The Cackler was wearing earplugs. The superhero conjured up a plan to fart instead of burp. So he tried to fart as loud as his burps and he did and The Cackler fainted. There was a horrible stench for two days.

Mehjabeen Kamran (11)
Quwwat-Ul-Islam Girls' School, Forest Gate

The Hungry Wizard

One day there was a very, very hungry wizard and his name was Billy Pig. Billy was a clumsy wizard. He did not know any spells. So he got his mum's spellbook. He accidentally said the wrong spell and lots and lots of food splurted out from the wall. The wizard licked his lips and ate all the food. Cakes, burgers, pizza, everything. Slowly and slowly he started blowing up. He was so fat. Billy's sister came to the room with a huge needle and poked him in the tummy. Billy said, "I am still super, super hungry."

Farhat Hoque (11)
Quwwat-Ul-Islam Girls' School, Forest Gate

The Talkative Unicorn Lost Her Precious Voice!

In Ridiculous Land there lived a unicorn and her best friend the pizza. They are both very, very talkative. They talked so much. They would start in the morning and all the way to the evening, they would even talk in their sleep! One day the unicorn couldn't talk, she tried and tried. She then looked under her chair like pizza told her to but she couldn't.

Sajeeha Sajjad (10)
Quwwat-Ul-Islam Girls' School, Forest Gate

Thomas, John And The Dragon

Once upon a time, there was a boy called Thomas and he lived with his friend John. They lived in a desert in the middle of Texas. The next day they said to their dad, "Can we have a pet dragon?" Their dad said, "Yes." So they got one. It was red and breathed fire, it was dangerous. Their dad was the king. A few days after they woke up and the dragon was gone. So they got dressed as fast as they could, they went to the pet sitting place and their dragon wasn't there at all.

Amelia Harrison-Blezard (9)
St John's CE Primary School, Bierley

The Rabbit Who Wanted To Be A Wolf's Friend

One day there was a rabbit who was lonely. All she wanted was a friend. The next day she saw a wolf. The wolf was called ask and he was dark grey and black. She saw a badger and the wolf ate it. The rabbit wanted to change the wolf to a good wolf. After two weeks of talking to the wolf, they both went on a trip to London city centre. The wolf nearly got started on so he ran back to the rabbit. When they got back, the wolf chased the rabbit and it got stuck. So sad.

Evie Theabould (10)
St John's CE Primary School, Bierley

Death (Top To Bottom) Life (Bottom To Top)

I am the last panda
I refuse to believe that
Humans can change their ways
this may shock you, but
'People care'
Is a lie
The damage is now irreversible
In time, people will say
It is true that
Greed
Is more important than
Kindness
I will tell you this
Once upon a time
Animals were sacred
There is no hope
People will tell me
I cannot believe
My kind will survive

Mia Dutton (9)
St John's CE Primary School, Bierley

The Naughty Scientist

The naughty scientist was busy in his lab. He was making a cotton candy monster so he could destroy the ice cream factory, so no one had any more ice cream. The monster had grown as tall as the Empire State building. He was heading for the ice cream factory. *Boom!* No more ice cream! But then the monster destroyed the whole town and almost the whole world! The naughty scientist said, "Yes my creature, destroy everything!" The monster felt a bit weird he felt like he could explode! *Bang!* The monster did! His creator said, "Noo, why?"

Olivia Willett Stewart (9)
St Patrick's Catholic Primary School, Heysham

The Evil Scientist

Once a scientist made a potion, he thought, *I wonder what my potion will do?* After drinking the purple potion it made him evil! He wanted to make massive monsters. He only knew one spell abracadabra then *boom!* A massive monster appeared, the evil scientist created him to scare all the people in the city. He watched it on the news. The monster returned to the lab and the scientist accidentally got the good potion and poured it on the monster. He turned good and splashed the potion on the scientists head. The evil scientist became the angel scientist.

Kyle Mitchell (8)

St Patrick's Catholic Primary School, Heysham

The Lazy Doctor

Once in a hospital, there was a doctor. The doctor was extremely lazy. He was always asleep for ages. Someone appeared in the hospital and said, "I'm so sick please help me!" The doctor didn't do anything, he was still silent but snoring loudly. The patients tried so hard to wake him up but nothing worked. "What shall we do? We are so ill." Something crazy happened, the doctor started to sleep fight and someone ill got hurt. The patient said, "No, stop!" Nothing happened. Finally, he woke up, so he could help out. Hurray!

Frankie Hobson (7)
St Patrick's Catholic Primary School, Heysham

The Extremely Stinky Rabbit

It all started with a cute little bunny which kept growing. He soon needed a new cage! One pitch-black night the rabbit escaped through the fence. He stayed out all night, he was scared.

Next morning the rabbit saw a little girl skipping down the path. She said, "Hello, I'm Ellie, why are you so smelly?" Ellie took him home and named him Luna. They walked inside, Mum saw the rabbit and said, "Why do you want him, he is smelly!" But Ellie didn't care, she loved him. She played with him all day. "I love you."

Laura-Kate Barker (8)
St Patrick's Catholic Primary School, Heysham

The Poorly Toilet

Once upon a time lived a poorly toilet and it was puking up badly, it was really, really, really, really poorly now. Its mum, dad, brother and sister said the pipes needed to be flushed. It was crying, they needed to get medicine for it so it could get better. Dad said, "Mum just nip to the shop and get some medicine please." This made the toilet well and truly sick. It was so, so poorly that they took it to the doctor.

"Yep it's burning up," said the doctor. Finally, the toilet got better and everyone cheered.

Cheryl Bamford (9)
St Patrick's Catholic Primary School, Heysham

Magical Pizza

It all started on a strange night when the chef made a pizza for himself. A special pizza but the pizza wasn't cooking. So he sat down. Suddenly, the pizza was dancing around. He thought he heard a sound but it must have been his imagination. He heard a *bang!* Again he checked the pizza, the pizza was cooking now. *Ding!* "It's ready," he said. He got the pizza out. "I'll call this the magical pizza, they will all love my idea." What he didn't know was that the pizza was magical.

Keisha Gray (8)
St Patrick's Catholic Primary School, Heysham

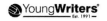
The Wizard Destroys Trump's House

Once upon a time on a lovely bright morning, a lazy old wizard woke up and fell out his bed! He said, "I bumped my head, ouch!" There was a portal in his van so he went in. "Whaat!" the wizard said. He saw Donald Trump's guard, he stole his cigarette and blew up Trump's office but the wizard had fire on his head. He put his head in the toilet. Trump found out and chased him. The wizard stole his limo. Donald Trump got in his car. The wizard went to the football pitch and ran through the portal.

Bob Howard (8)
St Patrick's Catholic Primary School, Heysham

The Terrifying Doctor

I had to go to the doctor but I had to see Doctor Terrifying. Some people say that he is an alien other people say that he is a small scary doctor who is a fish and alien disguised as a human. Here we go. "Hi Doctor Terrifying."

"Hi William."

"Are you going to eat me?"

"Yes!" said Doctor Terrifying. Then he transformed into a fish, alien, dog, cat, cow, pig and human. I ran as fast as I could. I fell over and then got back up, I ran outside the hospital and then...

William Featon (9)

St Patrick's Catholic Primary School, Heysham

Fartman's Weird Journey!

Once there lived a superhero called Fartman and he lived in his flat. Suddenly, his cape flew out the window! So he had to go after it, unfortunately, he couldn't fly. So he had to drive his rubbish Ford. All of a sudden, the cape stopped so Fartman had to stop too! Then, the cape landed. Now Fartman was really surprised. So Fartman grabbed his cape and went home. He figured out that his oven was broken so he had to fix that, so after that, he was pretty tired, so he decided to take a little rest for now.

Oliver Loughhead (9)
St Patrick's Catholic Primary School, Heysham

Rude Robot

I was minding my own business then suddenly I smelt something disgusting like a fart. It was my rude robot, he really is a stinky robot. They went on an adventure then they went to Buckingham Palace to see the Queen. Then they killed the Queen's guard. The Queen called the police so they could be arrested for 1000 days and only have glop and garbage water and clean the toilets with poo all over them. After 1000 days the rude robot was let out of prison and when he got home he was grounded for a year.

Zach Moorehouse (9)

St Patrick's Catholic Primary School, Heysham

Terrifying Wizard

I was sleeping in my comfy bed when all of a sudden I got dragged out of my bed. It was a terrifying wizard! He looked more terrifying and uglier than me. "I came here to take all your toys! You don't deserve them!" At that moment I really needed to go to the toilet so that didn't help. "Alright little girl to make it easier give me at least one toy, but it has to be new!" I took an old toy and gave it to the wizard hoping he wouldn't notice. Did the wizard notice the toy?

Alicia Dyminski (9)
St Patrick's Catholic Primary School, Heysham

Trump's Gangsta Foot

One morning in May the Gangsta Foot wakes up and goes downstairs to get a drink. Suddenly, Trump wakes up then goes downstairs to get a ladder to go upstairs. He then gets dressed and goes to the pub. He jumps on the table and dances on it and then runs out of the pub. He goes home and Gangsta Foot gets lost! Some people have a disco and he joins in. He hangs off the disco ball, it is scary. Gangsta Foot has a cigarette and gets a tattoo of a gangsta and then goes home.

Nathan Allison (8)
St Patrick's Catholic Primary School, Heysham

The Hungry Teacher!

Once there was a hungry teacher. She ate everything she saw, she emptied out the cupboards. She ate every day and night. One day she ate something horrible that was rotten fish, so she stopped eating everything. One day the children saw a pile of bones in the classroom, the children shivered and went back a little. The children ran to get a doctor. The doctor came and said, "Leave it there, we can't do anything." But she came back to live, it was scary.

Ruth Welch (8)
St Patrick's Catholic Primary School, Heysham

The Evil Ninja

One day a trained ninja turned evil! He sneaked into a bank. He took the guards out who were protecting the vault. He went in disguise and spent the money on a mansion with a bunker in the backyard. He hired professional guards to protect his mansion. One pitch-black night he went to rob the bank again, there was £200,000,000 in the silver vault. He crawled in the hot vent and claimed the money and ran out. The ninja woke up and it was all a crazy dream!

Eoghan Gurr (7)
St Patrick's Catholic Primary School, Heysham

The Hungry Sister Sophie!

Sophie can't stop thinking about food! She always wants food and she has just eaten all of her tea! So she asked her mum if she could have a snack.
"Mum, can I have a snack?"
Mum said, "Not now because it's your bedtime!"
She said, "Awww, fine!"
The next morning Sophie said, "Mum can I have some breakfast now?"
Mum said, "Yes come get it then."
Sophie said, "Okay!"
Mum said, "Come on otherwise your going to be late for school, then you will be in trouble."
Sophie said, "Okay, I'm coming now Mum."

Summer Widdop (9)
Worth Valley Primary School, Keighley

Rotten Rex

Rex was just minding his own business while he worked when suddenly, his bottom began to speak. The whole class burst out with laughter, however the teacher was not amused. Eran (the bully) smirked, "The baby isn't just good at crying but also letting out gas! Wow! Amazing!" Eran said sarcastically. Rex left the room with an embarrassed look on his face. Eran slyly followed Rex. "Well, if it isn't the gas bomb," Eran snapped. "Go away, I've had enough!" Rex argued back. Suddenly, Eran flew off by using the power of farts. Rex was cured and will be forevermore.

Seraphim Weston (10)
Worth Valley Primary School, Keighley

Evil Robot!

"Wow! I'm evil. Run!"

I need to get out of here. Maybe if I headbutt the door it will open. OMG it opened. My head hurts, I wonder why? I'm out of the lab. I see a very big building, let's investigate. There are kids and adults. I'm going to take over. Lava powers activated. Oh no, too much, run! Oof, lava got me, some metal has come off.

"Get in the forest now!" Argh! I'm very scared. Not even scared, petrified! Why are the scientists chasing me? "Don't turn me off!"

"Don't you worry, I am."

"Nooooo!"

Gracie McDermid (9)

Worth Valley Primary School, Keighley

The Secret Door

The boy, Ben, found a door underneath his bed. For a while, he looked at it as if he had seen a ghost! Suddenly, he opened the door and found a note saying 'Go inside and your dreams will come true!' He didn't understand how but he went through anyway. Inside was a whole new world. He saw coughing cupcakes, talking tortillas and groovy granola. Soon this funny fantasy turned into a nightmare. Everyone started being horrible and made jokes about him. "Look at Mr Long Legs." Soon he woke up. "Yes it was only a dream, thank you."

Faith Evans (10)
Worth Valley Primary School, Keighley

The Clumsy Soldier

One dark morning, the green soldiers were training in their owner's bedroom when suddenly the red soldiers attacked. The clumsy soldier tried to get to cover but slipped and got laughed at, He was left alone. The clumsy soldier couldn't get up and the enemies were coming. Two tanks blew up behind and he heard screaming. It was up to him, the clumsy soldier. He grabbed a bomb (in the shape of toilet paper) from his back pocket and threw it, landing in the middle of the red soldiers. He heard screaming, coughing and running. He saved the soldiers' land.

Alex Binns (11)
Worth Valley Primary School, Keighley

Giddy Glue

Giddy Glue strikes again leaping from table to table. He was leaping that much he got himself lost. He thought he wouldn't find his way back. Sadly, he began to cry and he kept crying until he was found, which he thought wouldn't happen. Instead of sitting on the table to be used. Finally, he stopped crying as Caitlin whispered to me, "He is far too giddy."

I replied, "I agree." We turned our head and saw him dancing all over the table as well as singing. Then he started to leap around the classroom again and got lost.

Katie Lund (10)

Worth Valley Primary School, Keighley

The Hungry Handbag

It's a normal, sunny day, Lisa is getting ready to go out with her friends. She goes to pick up her handbag, it suddenly, comes alive and starts running towards her. It gets faster and faster. Lisa jumps on her bed, she can't find her phone anywhere. She screams as loud as she can no one comes. Luckily, she sees an open window near her bed, she jumps out and sees a taxi, gets in and drives away. The handbag jumps out and follows them. Lucy yelled, "Faster, faster, what is going to happen to me? Argh!" *Crash! Bang!* Silence!

Lily Rose Perigo (10)
Worth Valley Primary School, Keighley

Floating Fiona!

Fiona was just feeding the dog as usual. She carelessly strolled outside to put the rubbish in the bin. When all of a sudden, Fiona started to float into the light, blue sky. Fiona's shoes began to fall off! The wheelie bin began to roll down the drive then started floating. Out of nowhere, Fiona's dog came running and barking! Fiona's dog caught her shoes and jumped down. The bin started to fly into the sky. Fiona reached for the bin. To her surprise, she began to slow down, floating lower and lower. Did Fiona reach the ground?

Caitlin Kendall (11)
Worth Valley Primary School, Keighley

Harry The Horrifying Horse!

I was minding my own business (as I normally don't) feeding Harry when suddenly... Harry kicked me in the face. "Ha!" screamed Harry out of nowhere. A fart blew out of Harry's nan's earhole, blowing me to China where I caught chickenpox. The Chinese doctor gave me tablets but there it was on Harry. The Coronavirus! We sailed him to China but we were too late, he turned into a centaur. So then I chopped off Harry's head and then flushed his head down the toilet, I gave him a sea slug to cure him but then he died!

Georgia Kershaw (11)
Worth Valley Primary School, Keighley

102

Fiesty Bubblegum

One fine day, Bob was out. Bob found bubblegum so he bought it. As he made his way home he happily chewed the gum. Suddenly, he felt a growing inside his mouth. He spat the gum out. It started to choke as it could smell peanut butter. Then over grown bubble tried to swallow whole streets. You could hear the screams of people, some people started throwing things. A girl threw peanut butter, it started to choke again. Everyone who had peanut butter started throwing it. Soon it had suffocated and died and fell as a small gum.

Darcy Carter (10)
Worth Valley Primary School, Keighley

The Flying Boxman

One day The Boxman was in his box when all of a sudden he started to float. Then he noticed he was still in his box then *bang* it smashed through the roof and he went up and up and up until he was higher than the clouds. Suddenly he felt a cold breeze on him, it was a rescue helicopter. "Jump onto the ladder," said the pilot. So he tried but couldn't, the pilot put the ladder longer then he shuffled over to them a little bit. "Finally, I'm saved!" Then the helicopter took him home.

Kaitlyn Smith (11)
Worth Valley Primary School, Keighley

The Monster Problem

One stormy night, she heard a noise coming from underneath her bed. It was a monster called Jeff. The young girl was called Grace, she was really scared because Jeff tickled her feet. After a while of talking they became best friends. Her mum and dad were really shocked they phoned the police. The police put it in a newspaper and on the news. Everyone read it! She became rich and very popular. Thankfully months later, after Grace was rich and popular she bought a new house, which was really big. It was really good!

Grace Halifax (10)
Worth Valley Primary School, Keighley

The Very Lazy Toilet

So I sat down and wondered what the snoring was and I began to investigate. I called the police. They said, "We can't help you." So I called the army, they said the same thing. So I called Area 51. They said, "Yes, we can help you."
We searched and searched until my toilet woke up! We caught it, put it in the van and drove and drove until we got there. We went in. I saw aliens and they saw me. We put the alien toilet in a titanium sealed door and it fell asleep again on a sofa.

Sam Robb (10)
Worth Valley Primary School, Keighley

Clumsy Guardian

I was protecting the stone when I slipped. The field was too slippery to fight in. *Bang!* I fell flat on my back. Thanos had the infinity stone in his grasp. I struggled to get up. *This is it*, I thought, *it's the end of Earth.* Finally, I got up and became stable. I launched myself at Thanos however he dodged my attack. I came up with the perfect plan. I could sneak up on him. Yes, it worked. Thanos slipped and I got away with the stone. I ran and ran until I got to my friends.

Casey Walker (11)
Worth Valley Primary School, Keighley

The Hairy Chef

The hairy chef got up and got dressed, he walked to work. At the restaurant, he was making spaghetti bolognese but fell over his long hairy toe. He tripped and fell and broke his arm. The kitchen was a big mess, he had to go to hospital. The doctor put a cast on his arm after an X-ray. He cut his hairy toes so it wouldn't happen again. He was happy, his friends came over to dance all night. In the morning he was surprised, he saw a hairy spider. He screamed and said, "Ha I have got you now!"

Paige Price (10)
Worth Valley Primary School, Keighley

Rude Chef

One early morning a very rude chef was in his cafe. A girl and boy were in the cafe too and he stood on a table serving food and he was also singing and dancing (he was really bad) Everyone was shouting boo and shh. Then he jumped off the table and said, "If you say boo or shh again you will get out of my cafe!" Everyone left as fast as they could. *How rude* he thought. "I just got upset, come back please I'll give you free food and drinks! Please come back, please!"

Maisie Smith (9)

Worth Valley Primary School, Keighley

The Grumbling Chef

Hey what are you doing here? That doesn't matter. Hi, I am the grumbling chef and I hate my job. My boss says to me, "Do the washing up, make food, don't be lazy." I am going to make my boss pay today, I will call my girlfriend and tell her to say she loved the food and walk out. Oh here she is now. Haha, my boss looks so mad. I am going to tell him, "Hey boss I quit, bye."

Ahh, finally home. I'm going to look for a better job. It was funny that he was mad.

Courtnie Sinfield (10)
Worth Valley Primary School, Keighley

Clumsy Banana

It was two aside and there were three minutes left, suddenly, the ball was flying through the air with a mighty kick. The fans were roaring furiously when the striker possed the ball in his grip. Running into the box with seconds to spare, he kicked it. With a through push, it swung to the top corner of the goal. Ten minutes passed and it became 3-2, he knew he had to win this one game of football or he'd be cut up. He won the game with ease and scored multiple goals. His team loved him!

Tomas Smith (11)
Worth Valley Primary School, Keighley

The Silly Dog

One sunny and boring day, I woke up to my owner hugging me. I heard him say, "Aw, you're so cute!" he explained. I saw Ice (she normally steals my treats) lying down sadly and I didn't want her to feel left out. I looked back at my treat, wait Ice took it! She stole my treat! Luckily owner gave me another treat, yay! My owner placed me down, I went to give her my treat. I love Ice so much. I wish she had more love, it's like my owner doesn't play with her.

Ellie Simpson (10)
Worth Valley Primary School, Keighley

The Horrible Handbag

One frosty school morning Sienna saw a black bag with gems. Sienna walked faster to the bag. When she was next to the bag she picked it up when she had it she felt strange. After school she took it home, then her mother called her to have her dinner. She went back to her room it was messy. She was in disbelief this went on for weeks, along with pulling her hair, tripping her over and eating her homework, she decided that she didn't want it anymore so she threw it in the fire.

Isabelle Whitaker (10)
Worth Valley Primary School, Keighley

Fly Away Bathtub

Suddenly Miss Lodge's bathtub zoomed out of her home, she was terrified. Thirty minutes went by. She was just doing her hair but she did not know that 1000 people were watching her, she did not realise until kids started shouting at her. She started to scream. When the newsman came she shouted, "Turn off that camera!"

"No, this will go viral and you look nice," replied the man. A horse went by, she was extraordinary, and then it landed on a hill.

Cody Morphet (11)
Worth Valley Primary School, Keighley

Stinky Toilet

One day there was a very stinky toilet. A girl called Sarah couldn't handle the smell it was too pungent. So she decided to clean the bathroom. Until she was just about to mop the floor she slipped into the toilet. Her phone rang. "Hello," she said. When her friends got there they took loads of pictures and put them on social media. She finally got out of the toilet. People kept on calling her Stanky Fish but she didn't mind and laughed at herself.

Demi Walton (9)
Worth Valley Primary School, Keighley

Story Time

Hi everyone this my story. One day I ordered a pizza then out of nowhere my friend Joseph Banks burst through my door and commanded, "Drink this Wade!"' and I did. So when I went on my next mission I continuously started trumping and burping. The next day I saw it on the news so I thought it was my secret weapon and I used it on a ton of the bad guys. I needed to stop! I couldn't so I told everyone to wear a gas mask and so they did.

Kaine Foster-Smith (10)
Worth Valley Primary School, Keighley

Welcome To Planet...

Once upon a time a greedy toot called, well, Toot, was very greedy because he got created by a kid while being at home. Toot escaped and ate everyone's food. After that he had a great big toot! The toot infected an active meteor! Disgusting! Suddenly the big rock, whatever you call it, fell and polluted the planet which in ten hours killed the whole planet! "Upsy daisy Toot, what a mess you've made.

Malachi Byrne (10)
Worth Valley Primary School, Keighley

YoungWriters®
— Est. 1991 —

YOUNG WRITERS INFORMATION

We hope you have enjoyed reading this book – and that you will continue to in the coming years.

If you're a young writer who enjoys reading and creative writing, or the parent of an enthusiastic poet or story writer, do visit our website **www.youngwriters.co.uk**. Here you will find free competitions, workshops and games, as well as recommended reads, a poetry glossary and our blog. There's lots to keep budding writers motivated to write!

If you would like to order further copies of this book, or any of our other titles, then please give us a call or order via your online account.

Young Writers
Remus House
Coltsfoot Drive
Peterborough
PE2 9BF
(01733) 890066
info@youngwriters.co.uk

Join in the conversation!
Tips, news, giveaways and much more!

 YoungWritersUK    @YoungWritersCW